ALSO BY PATRICK SÜSKIND

The Pigeon

Perfume

ALSO BY SEMPÉ

Par Avion

Mr. Summer's Story

PATRICK SÜSKIND

Mr. Summer's Story

WITH ILLUSTRATIONS BY SEMPÉ

Translated from the German by
John E. Woods

ALFRED A. KNOPF   NEW YORK   1993

THIS IS A BORZOI BOOK
PUBLISHED BY ALFRED A. KNOPF, INC.

Copyright © 1993 by Alfred A. Knopf, Inc.

Originally published in Switzerland as *Die Geschichte von Herrn Sommer* by Diogenes Verlag AG, Zurich.
Copyright © 1991 by Diogenes Verlag.

Library of Congress Cataloging-in-Publication Data
Süskind, Patrick.
[Geschichte von Herrn Sommer. English]
Mr. Summer's story / Patrick Süskind ; with illustrations by Sempé;
translated from the German by John E. Woods.—1st American ed.
p. cm.
Translation of: Die Geschichte von Herrn Sommer.
ISBN 0-679-41995-0
I. Title.
PT2681.U74G4713   1993
833'.914—dc20   92-19716   CIP

Manufactured in Mexico
FIRST AMERICAN EDITION

Mr. Summer's Story

In the days when I was still climbing trees—long, long ago, years, decades ago, I stood only a tad over three-foot-three, wore size-eleven shoes, and was so light I could fly—no, I'm not lying, I really could fly back then—or at least almost, or let's say it would actually have been within my power to fly in those days, if only I had truly wanted to and had tried really hard, because . . . I can recall very clearly that one time I came within an inch of flying, it was in autumn, my first year in school, I was on my way home, and the wind was blowing so strong that even without spreading my arms, I could lean way forward against it like a ski-jumper, or farther even, without falling over . . . and when I ran against the wind, down across the meadows of School Hill—our school, you see, was on a little hill outside the village—just by pushing myself off the least bit and spreading my arms wide, the wind lifted me up, and without even

3

trying I could leap five, ten feet high and bound forward thirty, forty feet—well, maybe not quite that far and not quite that high, what difference does it make!—but at least I *almost* flew, and if I had unbuttoned my coat and held it tight in both hands, spreading it like wings, why, the wind would have lifted me off for good, and easy as anything I could have sailed off School Hill, out across the valley to the woods and down to the lake, where our house was, and to the boundless amazement of my father, my mother, my sister, and my brother, who were all much too old and too heavy by then to fly, I would have traced an elegant curve above our yard and then floated out over the lake, almost to the far shore, and drifted gently at last back home, just in time for lunch.

But I didn't unbutton my coat and I didn't really fly. Not because I was afraid of flying, but because I didn't know how or where or even if I would be able to land again. The terrace in front of our house was too hard, our yard too small, the water in the lake too cold for a landing. Taking off—

that was no problem. But how did you get back down?

It was the same with climbing trees—there was no real difficulty in getting up. You saw the branch ahead of you, you could feel it in your hand and test its strength before pulling yourself up and setting your foot on it. But climbing back down, you couldn't see anything and had to poke around more or less blindly with your foot, trying to find firm footing on the branch below, and all too often the footing wasn't firm at all, but brittle or slick, and you slipped or the branch cracked underneath you, and if you weren't holding tight to another branch with both hands, you fell to the ground like a stone, obeying the laws of falling bodies, which were discovered by the Italian scientist Galileo Galilei almost four hundred years ago and are still valid today.

My worst fall happened during that same first year of school. It began fifteen feet up in a fir tree, proceeded exactly according to Galileo's first law of falling bodies, which says that the distance traveled is equal to one-half the product of the

gravitational constant and the time squared ($d = \frac{1}{2}g \cdot t^2$), and therefore lasted exactly 0.9578262 seconds. That is an extremely short time. It's less time than you need to count from twenty-one to twenty-two, even less time than you need to spit out the word "twenty-one"! It all happened so incredibly fast that I couldn't spread my arms or unbutton my coat and use it as a parachute, so fast that it never occurred to me I could save myself by flying instead of falling—I didn't think a single thought during those 0.9578262 seconds, and before I even realized *that* I was falling, I had crashed onto the forest floor at a final speed—according to Galileo's second law of falling bodies ($v = g \cdot t$)—of a little more than 20.5 miles per hour, crashed so violently in fact that the back of my head broke a branch as thick as my arm. The force involved here is called gravity. It is what holds the world's core together. But it has a quirk, too—it attracts everything, large or small, to itself with brutal force, and we seem to be freed from the tug of its halter only when resting in the womb or swimming suspended underwater. My fall left me

8

with that elementary insight, and a large bump. The bump disappeared in a few weeks, but as the years passed, whenever the weather changed, especially if snow was in the air, I would notice a curious tingling and throbbing in the same spot where the bump once was. And now, almost forty years later, the back of my head is a trusty barometer and I am better than the weather bureau when it comes to predicting if it will rain or snow tomorrow, if the sun will shine, or if a storm is brewing. I also think that a certain confusion and lack of concentration I've noticed of late is an aftereffect of my fall from the fir tree. For example, I find it increasingly difficult to stick to my subject, to express an idea briefly and succinctly, and when I'm telling a story like this one, I have to be damn careful not to lose the thread, otherwise I wander off into a thousand details, until finally I no longer know what it was I wanted to talk about.

And so in the days when I was still climbing trees—lots of them, I was good at it, I didn't always fall! I could even climb trees that didn't have lower branches, so that I had to shimmy up the bare trunk, and I could climb from one tree to another, and I built crow's nests, so many I lost count, and once even a real tree house, with a roof and windows and a carpet, deep in the woods, about thirty feet up—oh, I think I spent most of my childhood in trees, I ate and read and wrote and slept in trees, I learned my English vocabulary words up there, and my irregular Latin verbs and mathematical formulas and the laws of physics, like Galileo's laws of falling bodies—did my homework, all of it, written and oral, up in trees, and I loved to pee from up there, too, in long, high arcs splattering down through leaves and needles.

It was peaceful up in the trees, and you were left in peace. You weren't interrupted by your mother's calling you, or disturbed by your older brother's conscripting you, there was only the wind and the rustle of leaves and the soft creaking of boughs . . . and the view, the marvelous, wide view: I could look out beyond our house and yard, beyond other houses and yards, across the lake and the countryside beyond the lake to the mountains, and from the treetops I could watch the sun set each evening, watch it linger behind the mountains long after it had set for people down on the ground. It was almost like flying. Not quite so adventurous, not quite so elegant, perhaps, but a good substitute for flying all the same, especially because I was getting older now, stood four feet tall and weighed fifty pounds, which was simply too heavy for flying, even if a regular storm had been blowing and I had unbuttoned my coat and held it out wide. But I could climb trees—or so I thought then—all my life. Even as a rickety, doddering old man of a hundred and twenty, I would sit up there, at the top of an elm, or beech, or fir, like an ancient monkey rocking softly in the wind, gazing out over the land, across the lake, and beyond the mountains. . . .

But what am I doing talking about flying and climbing trees! Babbling on about Galileo's laws of falling bodies and the barometric spot at the back of my head that gets me so confused! When what I really want to do is something entirely different: to tell the story of Mr. Summer—if that's even possible, since there was no real story, there was only

that strange man, who crossed my path a few times during the course of his life—or would it be better to say during the walk of his life? The best thing, then, is to begin all over again.

In the days when I was still climbing trees, there lived in our village . . . or rather, not in our village, in Lower Lake, but in the next village of Upper Lake, though it wasn't easy to tell them apart, because Lower Lake and Upper Lake and all the other villages weren't strictly separated, but were set in a row along the lakeshore with no apparent beginning or end, like a slender chain of gardens and homes, farms and boathouses . . . So, then, there lived by the lake, barely a mile from our house, a man named Mr. Summer. No one knew Mr. Summer's first name, if it was Peter or Paul or Henry or Francis Xavier, or if he might not be Dr. Summer or Professor Summer, or Professor Dr. Summer—everyone knew him simply as "Mr. Summer." And no one knew if Mr. Summer had a job, or if he had ever had one. They knew only that *Mrs.* Summer had a job, that she was a doll-maker by profession. Day in, day out, she sat in their apartment—in the basement of the house owned by Stanglmeier, the housepainter— and made little dolls out of sawdust, wool, and other fabrics. Then she wrapped them all in a large package, which she took to the post office once a week. On her way back from the post office she stopped at the grocer's, the baker's, the butcher's, and the vegetable stand, one after the other, and returned home with four shopping bags stuffed full, and never left her apartment for another week, and made more dolls. The Summers had simply arrived in town one day, she on the bus, he on foot—and had been there ever since. They had no children, no relatives, and they never had any visitors.

Although people knew almost nothing about them, and in particular about Mr. Summer, it can be justly claimed that in those days Mr. Summer was the best-known man in the whole county. Within a radius of forty miles around the lake, there was not a man, woman, or child—no, not even a dog—who did not know Mr. Summer, because Mr. Summer was constantly on the move.

From early morning until late evening, Mr. Summer walked the countryside. Not a day passed that Mr. Summer was not on the go. Snow or hail, wind or gullywasher, searing sun or approaching hurricane—Mr. Summer was under way. He often left the house before sunrise, or so the fishermen said, who were out on the lake by four o'clock setting their nets, and he often did not return until late at night, when the moon stood high in the heavens. He could cover incredibly long distances within that time. It was nothing out of the ordinary for Mr. Summer to circle the lake in one day, a distance of some twenty five miles, or to walk to the county seat and back, six miles each way— never a problem for Mr. Summer. We children would be trudging sleepily to school at half past seven, and coming toward us we would see Mr. Summer, who had been under way for hours by then. We would walk home at noon, tired and hungry, and Mr. Summer would pass us at an energetic gait, and if I happened to look out my window at night before going to bed, I might very well see the tall, gaunt figure of Mr. Summer

hurrying past below on Shore Road, like a shadow.

He was easy to spot. Even at some distance, he was unmistakable. In winter he wore a long, black voluminous and strangely stiff coat, and with every step he made, it bounced around his body like an oversize husk—plus rubber boots and a ski hat with a pom-pom to cover his bald head. In summer, however—and for Mr. Summer, summer lasted from early March to late October, and was by far the largest part of the year—Mr. Summer wore a flat straw hat with a black band, a caramel-colored linen shirt, and caramel-colored shorts, and sticking out from them and looking almost absurdly skinny were long, sinewy legs, which seemed to be nothing but tendons and varicose veins and ended in a pair of bulky mountaineering boots. In March these legs were dazzling white, and the varicose veins clearly revealed an inky blue map of multi-tributaried rivers. Within a few weeks, however, his legs had turned a honey color, by July they were a glossy caramel-brown like his shirt and shorts, and by autumn sun, wind, and weather had tanned them so dark that there was no

2013 06 98

way to differentiate varicose veins, tendons, and muscles, and Mr. Summer's legs looked like gnarled branches of an old pine tree stripped of its bark—until in November they finally vanished under his long pants and his long black coat, where, removed from strangers' eyes, they found their way back to their original cheesy white by the next spring.

Mr. Summer carried two items with him, both winter and summer, and no one had ever seen him without them. The first was his walking stick and the second his backpack. The walking stick was no ordinary cane, but a long, slightly sinuous walnut staff, which reached higher than Mr. Summer's shoulder and served him as a kind of third leg and without which he would never have attained his phenomenal speed or covered those incredible distances, far exceeding those of a normal hiker. Every third step, Mr. Summer would pitch his staff forward with his right hand, brace it against the ground, and use it to propel himself forward with all his might, so that it looked as if his legs were merely gliding and that his right arm supplied the actual thrust, which was transmitted to the ground by the staff—rather like a river boatman poling his barge through the water. The backpack, however, was always empty, or almost empty, because it contained—as far as anyone knew—nothing except Mr. Summer's sandwich and a folded hip-length rubber cape with a hood, which Mr. Summer slipped on if he was surprised by rain during his walk.

And where did his wanderings lead him? What was the goal of his endless marches? For what reason and to what purpose did Mr. Summer race through the countryside for twelve, fourteen, sixteen hours a day? No one knew.

It was shortly after the war when the Summers settled in the village, and at that time no one took special notice of such long walks, because in those days everyone walked around with backpacks. There was no gas, no one had a car, and the bus ran only once a day. There was nothing to heat with, nothing to eat, and it often required hikes of several hours to find a couple of eggs or potatoes, or some flour or a pound or two of coal, even stationery or razor blades, and then you had to lug your prize home in a backpack or wheelbarrow. But within a few years, you could buy everything in the village, get your coal delivered, take a bus five times a day. And within a few more years, the butcher had his own car, then the mayor, then the dentist, and Stanglmeier, the housepainter, rode a motorcycle and his son had a motorbike. The bus still stopped three times a day, and no one would have thought of walking four hours to the county seat to take care of an errand or get his passport renewed. No one except Mr. Summer. Just as he always had, Mr. Summer walked. Early in the morning he buckled on his backpack, took his staff in hand, and hurried off across fields and meadows, down main roads and byways, through woods and around the lake, into town and back, from village to village . . . until late in the evening.

But the remarkable thing was that he never took care of any business. He delivered nothing, he bought nothing. His backpack was always empty, except for his sandwich and his cape. He never went to the post office or the courthouse, he left

that to his wife. He paid no visits, he never stopped anywhere. When he went into town, he didn't drop in somewhere for a bite to eat or a quick drink, he never even sat down on a bench to rest for a minute, but simply turned on his heels and hurried home, or wherever he was headed. If you asked, "Where have you been, Mr. Summer?" or "Where are you going?" he impatiently shook his head as if he had a fly on his nose, and mumbled something to himself that you either did not understand at all, or just bits and pieces of it that sounded like: "Gottahurryupschoolhillnow . . . quicklaparoundthelake . . . havtagetintotowntoday . . . inanawfulhurry . . . notasecondtospare . . ." and before you could say, "Pardon? What? Where?" he had already given a sturdy poke with his staff and scooted away.

Only once did I ever hear Mr. Summer utter a complete sentence—a clear, precise, unambiguous sentence, which I never forgot and which rings in my ears even today. It was on a Sunday afternoon at the end of July, during a terrible storm. The day had begun well enough, with radiant sunshine and barely a cloud in the sky, and at noon it was still so hot that all you wanted to do was drink iced tea with lemon. As he often did on Sunday, my father had taken me to the horse races. He went every Sunday. Not to bet, by the way—I would like to make special note of that—but purely out of love of the sport. Although he had never sat on a horse in his life, he was an ardent, knowledgeable fan. For example, he had memorized the names of all the winners of the German Derby since 1869, and could list them backward and forward, as well as the names of the most important winners of both the English Derby and the French Prix de l'Arc de Triomphe since 1910. He knew which horses liked muddy tracks and which preferred dry, why older horses took hurdles well and why young ones never ran more than the mile, how much the jockey weighed and why the owner's wife attached a bow of red, green, and gold to her hat. His library on horses contained more than five hundred volumes, and toward the end of his life he even owned a horse—or more precisely, half a horse—for which, to my mother's horror, he paid six thousand marks just so he could watch it run wearing his colors—but that's another story, and I'll have to tell it some other time.

So we had been to the horse races. As we drove home in the late afternoon, it was still hot, hotter and more sultry than at midday, but a thin layer of haze now covered the sky. Leaden clouds edged in pus-yellow gathered in the west. After fifteen minutes, my father had to turn on his lights—the clouds had moved in so swiftly that they formed a kind of curtain across the horizon and cast bleak shadows over the land. Then several gusts swept down from the hills and spread in broad strokes across the fields of grain, as if combing them, and bushes and shrubs took fright. And at almost the same moment, the rain started, no, not rain, at first just single fat drops, as big as grapes, that smashed here and there against the asphalt and exploded on the hood and windshield. And then the storm burst. The papers later reported that it was the area's worst storm in twenty-two years. I can't say if that's true, because I was only seven at the time, but I do know that I've never experienced another storm like it in all my life, and certainly not from inside a car on a country road. The water no longer fell in drops, it fell from the sky in swaths. In no time the road was flooded. Our car plowed through water spurting like fountains, building solid walls on both sides, and the windshield was a panel of water, even though the wipers were banging frantically back and forth.

But it got even worse. Gradually the rain turned into hail, you heard it before you saw it, a shift from a whoosh to a harder, brighter clatter, and you could feel it in the chill invading the car. Then you saw the hailstones themselves, at first little pinheads, but soon pea-size, then marble-size, and finally swarms of smooth white balls that rattled against the hood, bouncing in a wild, jumbled flurry that made you dizzy. We couldn't have driven one yard farther, so my father pulled to the side of the road, and stopped—what am I saying, the side of the road, there was no road, much less a shoulder, or a field, or a tree, or anything else, you couldn't see more than five feet ahead, and in those five feet, all you saw were millions of icy billiard

balls tumbling through the air and bouncing off the car with a dreadful racket. It was so noisy inside the car that we couldn't talk. We were sitting inside a kettle or a timpani and a giant was beating a tattoo, and we just looked at each other in silence, shivering and hoping that our protective casing wouldn't be demolished.

It was over in two minutes. The hail stopped from one second to the next, the wind fell away. Only a silent, fine drizzle was falling now. The field of grain, which the wind had just combed, now lay trampled beside us. Only bare stalks still stood in a distant cornfield. The road itself seemed strewn with broken glass—as far as the eye could see, splinters of hail, fallen branches, scattered foliage and grain. And through the delicate veil of drizzle, there at the far end of the road, I saw a human figure wending its way. I told my father, and we both stared at the little, distant figure, and we both thought it a miracle that anyone could be traipsing along out there, that anything was even standing after the hail, when everything around us had been crushed and mowed flat. We drove off, the rubble of hail crunching beneath us. As we neared the figure, I recognized the shorts, the long, gnarled legs glistening with rain, the black rubber cape and under it the soft contours of a backpack, Mr. Summer's urgent gait.

We had caught up with him, and my father now told me to roll down the window—the air was icy out there. "Mr. Summer," he called, "get in! We'll take you with us," and I scrambled into the back-seat to make room for him. But Mr. Summer did not answer. He didn't even stop. He barely threw us a quick sidelong glance. With a thrust of his walnut staff, he rushed ahead, striding down the hail-strewn road. My father drove after him. "Mr. Summer!" he cried from the open window. "Do get in! In this awful weather! I'll take you home."

But Mr. Summer did not react. He marched grimly on. Though it did seem to me as if his lips were moving slightly, forming one of his indecipherable answers. But not a sound could be heard, and maybe his lips were just trembling from the cold. And then my father leaned way to the right—still steering the car alongside

Mr. Summer—opened the passenger door, and shouted, "Get in, for God's sake! You're drenched. You'll catch your death!"

Now, the expression "You'll catch your death" was very uncharacteristic for my father. I had never heard him say to anyone with any seriousness: "You'll catch your death." Whenever he heard or read the phrase "catch your death," he would be sure to explain, "The expression is a cliché, and a cliché—mark this now, for good and all!—is an idiom that has passed so often through the mouths and pens of every Tom, Dick, and Harry that it no longer means anything. It's the same thing," he would continue, having hit his stride, "it's just as stupid and meaningless as when you hear someone say, 'Have a cup of tea, my dear, it will do you good,' or 'How's our patient doing, Doctor? Do you think he'll pull through?' Such phrases do not come from real life, but from bad novels and stupid American films, and therefore—mark this now, for good and all!—I never want to hear them coming from your mouths."

That was my father's way of enlarging on sayings like "You'll catch your death." But now, as he drove down that hail-covered road in the drizzle, holding right alongside Mr. Summer, my father shouted that same old cliché from the open car door: "You'll catch your death!" And Mr. Summer pulled up short. I think he stopped in his tracks at the words "your death," and I mean so abruptly that my father had to slam on the brakes to keep from driving past him. And then Mr. Summer shifted his walnut staff from his right hand to his left, turned toward us, and pounding his staff on the ground several times in a kind of desperate gesture of defiance, he shouted these words in a loud, clear voice: "Why can't you just leave me in peace!" That was all he said. Just that one sentence. And at that he slammed the open car door shut, shifted his staff back into his right hand, and marched off without glancing to either side, without glancing back.

"The man is totally crazy," my father said.

As we passed him then, I watched his face through the back window. His eyes were fixed on the ground, but when he raised them every few steps and stared straight ahead for a moment to check his path, they seemed wide with horror. Water was running down his cheeks, dripping from his nose and chin. His mouth was slightly open. And I thought I saw his lips moving again. Maybe he was talking to himself as he walked along.

O ur Mr. Summer is claustrophobic," my
mother said as we all sat at supper, talking
about the storm and our encounter with Mr. Summer. "He suffers from severe claustrophobia, an
illness where you can't sit still in your own room."

"Strictly speaking, 'claustrophobia' means," my
father said—"that you can't sit still in your room,"
my mother said. "Dr. Luchterhand explained it all
in detail for me."

"The word 'claustrophobia' comes from Latin
and Greek," my father said, "as I'm sure Dr. Luchterhand knows quite well. It consists of two parts,
claustrum and *phobia*, whereby *claustrum* means something like 'closed' or 'locked'—as in our word
'closet,' or in the name of the town 'Klausen,'
which is 'Chiusa' in Italian, or 'Vaucluse' in French.
Who can give me another word with *claustrum*
hidden within it?"

"I can," my sister said. "I heard from Rita

Stanglmeier that Mr. Summer is constantly twitching. He twitches all over with muscle tics, he's antsy-pantsy, that's what Rita says. He sits down in a chair—and starts twitching. But as long as he's walking, he doesn't twitch, and that's why he always has to keep moving, so that no one can see him twitching."

"It's much the same with yearlings," my father said, "or two-year-olds, they twitch and quiver and tremble all over, they're so nervous the first time they go to the gate. Jockeys have their hands full getting them to break out. They do it all on their own later, of course, or they have to wear blinders. Who can tell me what 'break out' means?"

"Fiddlesticks!" my mother said. "If he'd gotten in the car, Mr. Summer could have twitched all he liked. A little twitching never bothered anyone."

"I'm afraid," my father said, "that Mr. Summer didn't get into the car with us because I used a cliché. I said: 'You'll catch your death!' I don't know how that could have happened to me. I'm sure he would have gotten in if I had used a less hackneyed phrase, for instance . . ."

"Nonsense," my mother said, "he didn't get in because he's claustrophobic, which means that if he can't sit in a room, he can't sit in a closed car, either. Ask Dr. Luchterhand. The minute he finds himself in a closed space—whether it's a car or a room—he's in awful straits."

"What does 'straits' mean?" I asked.

"Maybe," my brother said, who was five years older than I and had read all of Grimms' fairy tales by then, "maybe Mr. Summer is just like the runner in the story 'Six Who Made Their Way in the World,' who can circle the earth in a single day. But when he gets home he has to buckle up one leg in a strap, because otherwise he wouldn't be able to stand still."

"That's a possibility, too, of course," my father said. "Maybe Mr. Summer simply has one leg too many and that's why he has to keep walking. We should ask Dr. Luchterhand to buckle up one of his legs."

"Nonsense," my mother said, "he's claustrophobic, that's all, and there's no cure for claustrophobia."

The word claustrophobia comes
from Latin and Greek... means
something like "closed" or "locked."...
Claustrophobia is an illness
where you can't sit still in
your room.

As I lay in bed, that marvelous word kept going 'round and 'round in my head: *claustrophobia*. I spoke it aloud several times, so I wouldn't forget it. "Claustrophobia . . . claustrophobia . . . Mr. Summer suffers from claustrophobia. . . . That means he can't stay in his room. And because he can't stay in his room, he has to run around outside. It's because he's claustrophobic that he has to keep running around outside. . . . But if claustrophobic is the same thing as not-being-able-to-stay-in-your-room and not-being-able-to-stay-in-your-room is the same thing as having-to-run-around-outside, then having-to-run-around-outside is the same thing as claustrophobic . . . and so instead of using a big word like 'claustrophobic' you could just say 'having to run around outside.' But then that would mean that when my mother says, 'Our Mr. Summer has to keep running around outside because he's claustrophobic,' she could just as easily say, 'Our Mr. Summer has to keep running around outside because he has to keep running around outside.'. . ."

And that made me feel a little dizzy, and I tried

quickly to forget this crazy new word and everything connected with it. And instead I tried to imagine that Mr. Summer didn't suffer from anything or have to do anything, but that he simply ran around outside because he thought it was fun to run around outside, just like I thought it was fun to climb trees. And so Mr. Summer ran around outside simply to please himself, just for the fun of it, that was the whole thing, and all the confusing explanations and Latin words that adults came up with at supper were just as absurd as the fellow who buckled up one leg in the fairy tale "Six Who Made Their Way in the World."

But after a while, I couldn't help remembering Mr. Summer's face, the way I'd seen it through the back window, a face with rain running down it and a mouth half open and those giant eyes petrified with terror, and I thought: That's not how you look if you're having fun; no one who's doing something for the sheer pleasure of it makes a face like that. That's how someone looks when he's afraid, or when he's thirsty, so thirsty, right in the middle of a rainstorm, that he could drink a whole lake. And that made me feel dizzy again, and I tried as hard as I could to forget Mr. Summer's face, but the harder I tried to forget it the clearer it stood before my eyes. I could see every wrinkle, every crease, every drop of sweat and every drop of rain, the slightest twitch of his lips, which seemed to be murmuring something. And the murmur grew clearer and louder, and I understood Mr. Summer's voice, and it was pleading: "Why can't you just leave me in peace! Leave me in peace, in peace . . . !"

And only then could I separate him from my thoughts—it was his voice that helped. The face vanished, and I fell asleep almost at once.

There was a girl named Caroline Kueckelmann in my class. She had dark eyes, dark eyebrows, and dark brown hair tucked back on the right with a barrette. The down on the nape of her neck and in the little dimple under her earlobe glistened in the sun and sometimes rippled very gently in the breeze. When she laughed, in her marvelous husky voice, she would stretch her neck and tilt her head back, her whole face beaming with delight, her eyes almost closed. I could have gazed at that face forever, and I did gaze at it as often as I could, in class and during recess. But they were stolen glances, so no one would notice, not even Caroline, because I was very shy.

I was less shy in my dreams. I would take her by the hand then and lead her into the woods and climb trees with her. Sitting next to her on a branch, I would gaze into her face, very close, and tell her stories. And she simply had to laugh, tilting her head back, closing her eyes, and then I could blow softly on the nape of her neck, just behind her ear, where the down was. I dreamed dreams like that several times a week. They were beautiful dreams—I'm not complaining—but they were only dreams, and like all dreams not really emotionally satisfying. I would have given anything to have the real Caroline sitting beside me, just once, so that I could blow softly on the nape of her neck or wherever. . . . Sad to say, there was almost no chance it would ever happen, because like most of the other kids Caroline lived in Upper Lake—I was the only one from Lower Lake. Our paths parted just beyond the school gate, descended School Hill, and led across the meadows, diverging more and more, until finally, just before both roads vanished into the woods, I could no longer pick Caroline out from among the other kids. Sometimes, though, I could hear her laugh in the distance. If the weather was just right, and the wind was from the south, her husky laugh came drifting across the fields and accompanied me all the way home. But then, how often did we ever get a wind from the south?

One day—a Friday—a miracle happened. During recess Caroline came running over, stopped right in front of me, very close, and said, "Hey, listen! You always walk to Lower Lake by yourself, don't you?"

"Yes," I said.

"Well, on Monday, I'll walk with you. . . ."

And then she offered a long explanation, about how a friend of her mother's lived in Lower Lake, and that her mother would pick her up at the friend's house, and she would go home from there with her mother or with the friend or with her mother *and* the friend. . . . I don't remember, I've forgotten that part, I suppose I forgot it that day, too, the moment she said it, because I was so surprised, so overwhelmed by her saying, "On Monday, I'll walk with you!" that I was incapable of hearing anything else, all I wanted was that one marvelous sentence: "On Monday, I'll walk with you!"

The rest of the day, the whole weekend really, the words rang in my ears, they sounded glorious—what am I saying!—sounded more glorious than anything I'd ever read in Grimms' fairy tales, more glorious than the princess's promises in "The Frog King": "You may eat from my plate, you may sleep in my bed"; and I counted the days more impatiently than Rumpelstiltskin: "Brew today, tomorrow bake, and then the queen's child I'll take!" I felt like Hans in Luck and Brother Scamp and the King of the Golden Mountain all in one. . . . "On Monday, I'll walk with you!"

I made preparations. I spent Saturday and Sunday roaming the woods, searching for the perfect route. I wouldn't use the main road with Caroline, that much was certain from the start. She would learn my most secret paths, I would show her all the hidden sights. The splendors she would see on her way, on our way, to Lower Lake would make the road to Upper Lake fade from her memory.

After due consideration, I decided in favor of a route that turned off to the right just beyond the edge of the woods, led through a little ravine to a group of firs, then crossed a mossy clearing to a stand of hardwoods before making a steep descent to the lake. This route was embellished with no less than six special points of interest that I wanted to show Caroline, while providing expert commentary on each. These six were, in order:

(a) A transformer shed, property of the power company, still very near the road, from which came a constant hum, and on its door was a yellow sign with a bolt of red lightning and the warning: "Danger—Fatal—High Voltage!"

(b) A cluster of seven raspberry bushes, with ripe berries.

(c) A feeding station for deer—without hay at present, but at least there was a large salt lick.

(d) A tree from which people said an old Nazi had hung himself after the war.

(e) An anthill, almost three feet high and five feet across.

And finally, as the high point of the tour.

(f) A wonderful old beech tree, which I intended to climb with Caroline, as far as a sturdy fork about thirty feet up, there to enjoy with her the incomparable view across the lake, and to bend down and blow softly on the nape of her neck.

I stole cookies from our pantry, a glass of yogurt from the icebox, two apples and a bottle of currant juice from the cellar. On Sunday afternoon I packed it all in a shoe box, which I then stashed in the fork of the beech tree so that we would have supplies. That evening in bed, I thought up the stories I would tell Caroline to amuse her and make her laugh, one for the walk, the other for our stopover in the beech tree. I turned the light on again, searched in the drawer of my nightstand for a little screwdriver, my most treasured possession, which I slipped into my schoolbag, planning to give it to her as we parted. Back in bed, I went over both stories again, rehearsed in detail my plans for the coming day, with several recaps of the stops along the way, from (a) to (f), and the place and moment when I would present the screwdriver, reviewed the contents of the shoe box, which was now out there in the woods, wedged in the sturdy branch and waiting for us—never was a rendezvous more carefully planned!—and finally yielded to slumber, to the accompaniment of her sweet words: "On Monday, I'll walk with you . . . on Monday, I'll walk with you . . ."

Monday was flawless. The sun shone gently, the sky was as clear and blue as water, blackbirds piped in the woods, and woodpeckers hammered till the sound echoed on all sides. Only now, on the way to school, did it occur to me that I hadn't even calculated what to do with Caroline in case of bad weather. My route from (a) to (f) would have been a catastrophe on a stormy, rainy day—with rumpled raspberry bushes, a grubby anthill, a mossy path squeaking underfoot, a slick beech tree that couldn't be climbed, and a box of supplies either blown away or turned soggy. I blissfully gave my fantasies of catastrophe free rein; they provided me with sweet, superfluous cares and an almost triumphant sense of my own good fortune. Not only had I paid no mind to the weather, but the weather itself had watched out for *me*! Not only was I to escort Caroline Kueckelmann today, but I had been given the extra treat of the most beautiful day of the year! I was Sunday's child. God had

sought me out, personally, and His gracious eye rested upon me now. Be careful—I thought—don't overdo it, despite the state of grace. Avoid making any mistakes now, getting too proud or too big for your britches, the way heroes in fairy tales always do, managing to destroy the good fortune they think is already theirs.

I walked faster. I didn't dare be late for school. I never behaved so well in class as I did that day. I wasn't about to give the teacher the least cause for keeping me after school. I was simultaneously meek as a lamb and eagle-eyed, busy as a beaver, a high-minded grind, the absolute model student. I did not look at Caroline even once, I forced myself not to, not yet, I wouldn't allow myself to do it, out of superstition maybe, as if I could lose her in the end by looking too soon.

When school was over, it turned out that the girls would have to stay for another hour, I don't remember why now, for a sewing class or something like that. At any rate, only we boys were dismissed. I did not regard this as a tragedy—on the contrary. It seemed to me a further test that I had to pass, and would pass, and it added a special touch of sanctification to my yearning to be with Caroline—we would wait for one another for a whole hour!

I waited at the fork in the road to Upper Lake and Lower Lake, not twenty yards beyond the school gate. A stone rose up from the earth at that spot, a smooth boulder left behind by a glacier. In the middle of the stone was a distinctive hoof-shaped indentation. People said that the imprint was from the devil's foot, that one day, time out of mind, he had stamped on the ground in a rage because farmers were building a church nearby. I sat down on the stone and passed the time by flicking with one finger at the little puddle of rainwater in the devil's hoofprint. The sun shone warm on my back, the sky was as clear and watery blue as before; I sat and waited and flicked and thought of nothing and felt indescribably satisfied with myself.

Then, at last, here came the girls. First a whole flood of them rushing past, and then, at the very end, Caroline. I stood up. She came over, her dark

hair swinging, the barrette bobbing on one strand at her forehead, she was wearing a lemon-yellow dress, I put my hand out to her, she stopped right in front of me, as close as on that day during recess, I wanted to take hold of her hand, pull her to me, most of all I would have liked to give her a hug and kiss her square on the mouth. She said, "Hey! Did you wait all this time for me?"

"Yes," I said.

"Listen. I won't be walking with you today. My mother's friend is sick, and my mother won't be visiting her, and my mother said that . . ."

A whole jumble of explanations followed, which I didn't even listen to, let alone try to remember, because suddenly my head felt so numb and I was so shaky on my legs, and the only thing I still recall is that after she finished her speech, all at once she turned around and ran off lemon-yellow in the direction of Upper Lake, trying to catch up with the other girls.

I started down School Hill for home. I must have walked very slowly, because when I finally reached the edge of the woods and automatically looked across to the faraway road to Upper Lake, there was no one in sight. I stopped, turned around, and gazed back at the rolling ridge of School Hill, where I had come from. The sun lay rich on the meadows, not the least shadow of wind passed over the grass. The whole landscape seemed rigid.

And then I saw a little dot in motion. A dot, at the far left of the woods, moving steadily toward the right, along the woods' edge, wandering up School Hill, and once at the top, it followed the rolling crestline toward the south. And although the dot looked as small as an ant against the blue background of sky, that was clearly a person walking up there, and I recognized Mr. Summer's three legs. As regular as seconds on a clock, his legs moved forward in tiny paces, and the distant dot edged its way along the horizon—like the slow yet quick passing of the big hand on a clock.

A year later I learned to ride a bike. That was none too soon, since I already stood four-foot-six, weighed seventy pounds, and wore size-thirteen shoes. But I had never had any special interest in learning to ride a bike. Forward motion that teetered along on nothing more than two slender wheels seemed profoundly unsafe to me, even mysterious, because no one could explain to me why a bike promptly fell over when at rest, that is, if someone wasn't holding on to it or hadn't braced or propped it against something—but would *not* fall over when a seventy-pound person sat on it and rode off without any kind of brace or prop. I was quite unfamiliar at the time with the mechanical laws behind this strange phenomenon, that is, the laws of axial rotation, and in particular the so-called conservation of rotational impulse, and even today I don't fully understand them, and I find the very term "conservation of rotational impulse" rather eerie and so bewildering that it makes the old spot at the back of my head start to tingle and throb.

Presumably I would never have learned to ride a bike if it had not proved absolutely necessary. But it became absolutely necessary because I was supposed to take piano lessons. And I could take piano lessons only with a piano teacher who lived at the other end of Upper Lake, a trip of more than an hour on foot, but only thirteen and a half minutes by bike—according to my brother's calculation.

This teacher, who had taught piano to my mother and my sister and my brother and practically every other soul in town who knew one key from another—whether on the parish organ or Rita Stanglmeier's accordion—this piano teacher's name was Maria Louisa Funkel, or better, *Miss*

Maria Louisa Funkel. She set great store by the "Miss," although in all my life I've never seen a female who looked less like a miss than Maria Louisa Funkel. She was old as the hills—white-haired, hunchbacked, shriveled, with a little black moustache, and no bosom at all. I know, because I once saw her in her undershirt—by mistake I arrived an hour early for my lesson and she was still taking her afternoon nap. There at the front door of her huge old villa she stood, wearing nothing but a skirt and an undershirt, and not a delicate, flimsy silk camisole that a lady might wear, but one of those old, tight-fitting, bare-shouldered cotton affairs, like the ones we boys wore for gym class, and her wrinkled arms dangled from her gym shirt, and her thin, leathery neck stuck up out of it—and the breast underneath was as flat and skinny as a chicken's. All the same, she insisted—as I said—on a "Miss" in front of "Funkel," because—as she often explained, though no one ever asked—gentlemen might think she was married, whereas she was a maiden lady, and still available. This was pure nonsense, of course, because there wasn't a

man in the world who would have married old, moustached, bosomless Maria Louisa Funkel.

In fact, Miss Funkel called herself "Miss Funkel" because she could not have called herself "Mrs. Funkel" if she had wanted to, since there already was a Mrs. Funkel . . . or perhaps I should say, there still was a Mrs. Funkel. Miss Funkel, you see, had a mother. And since I've already said that Miss Funkel was old as the hills, I don't know what I should say about Mrs. Funkel: an antique, a relic, a fossil, older than the hills. . . . I'm sure she was at least a hundred years old. Mrs. Funkel was so old that you would have to say she existed only in a very narrow sense of the word, was more like a piece of furniture or a dusty butterfly specimen or a fragile old vase than a human being of flesh and blood. She did not move, she did not speak. I don't know how much she heard or saw, and I never saw her do anything but sit. Silent, immobile, unnoticed, she sat in a wing chair in a far corner of the music room, right under a grandfather clock. Her summer dress was a web of white tulle, and in winter she was wrapped in black velvet, her head sticking up like a turtle's. On very rare occasions, however—when a pupil had learned an assigned piece especially well and could play his Czerny études without a mistake—Miss Funkel would move to the center of the room at the end of the session and bellow in the direction of the wing chair, "Ma!"—she called her mother "Ma"— "Ma! Give the boy a cookie, he played so beautifully!" And then you had to walk to the far corner of the room, stand in front of the wing chair, and hold your hand out to the old mummy. Then Miss Funkel would bellow again, "Give the boy a cookie, Ma!" And indescribably slowly, from somewhere within the web of tulle or black velvet, a trembling, bluish, ancient hand would emerge, delicate as glass. But the turtle head and eyes would ignore it, as it drifted off to the right, over the chair arm, to an end table with a bowl of cookies, extracted one—usually a square waffle cookie with creamy white filling—wandered slowly back over end table, chair arm, and lap, the cookie still clutched in its bony fingers, and laid it like a gold coin in your outstretched hand. Sometimes your

hand and the ancient fingertips would touch for a brief moment, and your blood would run cold, because you were expecting a hard, fishy touch, and instead it felt warm, even hot, incredibly gentle and feather-light, like a bird escaping from your hand, and in that fleeting moment, you shuddered. And stammered your "Thank you, Mrs. Funkel," and got out of there, out of that room, out of that gloomy house, out into fresh air and sunlight.

I don't know how long it took for me to learn the eerie art of riding a bike. I only know that, reluctant but doggedly diligent, I taught myself on my mother's bike, on a gently sloping path in the woods, where no one could see me. The narrow path had steep banks on both sides, so that I could prop myself against them whenever I had to, and even when I fell, it was into leaves or soft ground. And at some point, after many, many failed attempts, I was suddenly surprised to find I had the knack of it. Despite all my theoretical scruples and profound skepticism, I was propelling myself easily along on two wheels—feeling both startled and proud. I passed my driving test on our terrace and adjacent areas of lawn, in the presence of my assembled family, and earned applause from my parents and shrill laughter from my brother and sister. Afterward, my brother familiarized me with the most important traffic rules—the first being to keep always to the far right, right being defined as the side of the handlebars with the hand brake*—and from then on I rode all by my lonesome to Miss Funkel's for my weekly piano lesson, Wednesday afternoons from three to four. Of course, my brother's calculation of thirteen and a half minutes for covering the distance was out of the question. My brother was five years older than I and had a three-speed racer. Whereas I rode standing up on my mother's bike, which was much too big for me. Even after adjusting the seat to its lowest position, I couldn't sit and pedal at the same

---

*Even today, I depend on this pithy definition, especially when, in some moment of temporary confusion, I can no longer tell my right from my left. I simply picture bicycle handlebars, mentally apply the hand brake—and once again I have my bearings down perfectly. I would never get on a bicycle with brakes on both handlebars or—even worse!— on the left side.

time, but had either to sit or to pedal, a highly inefficient and tiring method, and also, as I well knew, a ridiculous sight to behold. I would pedal hard to get going, heave myself up onto the seat once I had picked up speed, and there I perched precariously, my legs spread wide or pulled up, until the bike had coasted almost to a stop, and only then would I climb back onto the still-rotating pedals and build up another head of steam. My lurching technique meant the ride from our house to Miss Funkel's villa, by way of Shore Road and through the village of Upper Lake, took twenty minutes—that is, if nothing happened along the way. But something usually happened. The problem was that although I could get on and off my bike, pedal, steer, and brake, I was incapable of passing anyone, of being passed, or of meeting anyone coming toward me. The moment I heard the faintest sound from the motor of an approaching car, whether behind or ahead of me, I would brake, get off, and wait until the car had passed. If other bikers came into view, I would stop and wait until they had passed. When passing a pedestrian, I would get off just before I caught up with him, run past pushing my bike, and start pedaling again only after I had left him well behind me. For bike-riding, I needed a perfectly open road before and behind me, and if possible no one around to watch. And finally, about halfway between Lower Lake and Upper Lake, there was Mrs. Hartlaub's dog, a nasty little terrier that liked to loiter beside the road and launch a yelping attack on anything on wheels. To avoid his attacks, you had to pull to the edge of the road, stop next to the fence, deftly perch yourself there by grabbing one of the pickets and pulling your legs up, and wait until Mrs. Hartlaub whistled and called the little beast off. It's no wonder, then, that under such circumstances it often took me more than twenty minutes to make it to the far end of Upper Lake, and so I got into the habit of leaving home at half past two, just to make sure I would arrive at Miss Funkel's more or less on time.

In noting that Miss Funkel occasionally directed her mother to reward a pupil with a cookie, I intentionally pointed out that this happened only very, very rarely. It was certainly not usual, because Miss Funkel was a strict teacher and hard to please. If you had been sloppy about learning your assigned piece or hit one wrong note after another when sight-reading, her face would turn bright red and she would begin rocking her head menacingly, poking you in the side with an elbow, snapping her fingers in the air, and then would suddenly let loose with a volley of bellowed abuse. The worst such scene happened to me about a year after I began lessons with her, and it so rattled me that I get upset recalling it even now.

I was late, about ten minutes late. Mrs. Hartlaub's terrier had driven me to the fence, I had met two oncoming cars, and I had had to pass four pedestrians. By the time I entered her house, Miss Funkel's face was red and she was pacing up and down the room, snapping her fingers in the air.

"Do you know what time it is?" she growled. I didn't answer. I didn't have a watch. I got my first watch on my thirteenth birthday.

"Look!" she shouted, snapping her fingers in the direction of the far corner, where Ma Funkel sat inert beneath the ticking grandfather clock. "It's a quarter past three! You've been dawdling again, haven't you?"

I started to stammer something about Mrs. Hartlaub's dog, but she didn't let me explain. "A dog!" she interrupted. "I knew it, playing with a dog! And probably stopped for ice cream. I know you boys too well. Always hanging around Mrs. Hirt's ice cream stand, thinking of nothing but licking an ice cream cone!"

That was terribly mean of her! To accuse me of buying ice cream at Mrs. Hirt's stand. When I didn't even get an allowance. My brother and his friends did things like that. They spent their whole allowance at Mrs. Hirt's ice cream stand. But not me! I had to beg and beg my mother or my sister for the money for every ice cream cone. And now I was being accused of hanging around Mrs. Hirt's ice cream stand, licking my life away, when in fact I had ridden my bike to my piano lesson, under very difficult, sweaty conditions. That was so mean of her that words simply failed me, and I began to cry.

"Stop sniveling!" Miss Funkel barked. "Get out your music and show me what you've learned. You probably haven't practiced again, either."

Sad to say, she wasn't all that wrong. Actually, I had barely gotten around to practicing in the last week, partly because I had other, more important things to do, partly because the études she'd given me were wretchedly hard, some kind of fugue, a canon, with right hand and left moving far apart, lingering out there, first one entering suddenly, then the other, with the most stubborn rhythms and odd intervals, and it sounded disgusting besides. The composer's name was Hassler, if I'm not mistaken—I hope he's rotting in hell.

All the same, I think I could have managed both pieces decently enough, if my nerves had not been totally undone by various episodes on my bike ride—primarily the attack by Mrs. Hartlaub's terrier—and by Miss Funkel's explosion once I got there. But now, trembling and sweating, my eyes blurred by tears, I sat at the piano, eighty-eight keys and Mr. Hassler's études before me, Miss Funkel behind, her angry breath blowing down my

72

neck . . . and I failed miserably. I got everything mixed up, bass and treble clefs, half notes and whole notes, quarter rests and eighth rests, left and right. I didn't even make it to the end of the first staff before keys and notes all burst into a kaleidoscope of tears and I dropped my arms to my sides and wept silently to myself.

"Jussst as I thought!" came the hiss behind me, and a fine vaporized shower of spit sprayed the back of my neck. "Jussst as I thought. Late for lessons and full of ice cream and excuses—that's your fine gentlemen for you! But practice their music—that they can't! Just wait, my boy, I'll teach you how to play it!" And with that she shot out from behind me, sat down next to me on the bench, grabbed my right hand in both of hers, seizing each finger, forcing one after the other onto the keys, just the way Mr. Hassler had composed it. "This one here! And this one here! And this one here! And the thumb here! And the middle finger here! And this one here! And this one here . . . !"

And when she finished with my right hand, it

was the left's turn, with the same method. "This one here! And this one here! And this one here . . .!"

She pressed on my fingers so savagely it was as if she were trying to knead the étude into my hands, note by note. It really hurt, and lasted for about half an hour. Then finally she let go, opened her notebook, and snapped, "You'll master it by next time, my boy, and not just with the music in front of you, but by heart, and allegro, or else!" Then she opened a thick four-handed score and slammed it on the music stand. "And now we'll play Diabelli for ten minutes, so that you can learn to sight-read. And don't you dare make a mistake!"

I nodded meekly and wiped the tears from my face with my sleeve. Diabelli—now, he was a friendly composer. He was no fugue-drudge like that unmerciful Hassler. Diabelli was easy to play, almost silly he was so easy, and yet somehow it managed to sound marvelous. I loved Diabelli, even though my sister sometimes said, "If you can't play the piano, you can always play Diabelli."

And so we played Diabelli four-handed, with Miss Funkel grinding out the bass on the left, and me playing unison treble with both hands on the right. It moved along quite jauntily for a while, my self-assurance gradually increasing, and I thanked the good Lord for having created the composer Anton Diabelli, and was so relieved that I forgot the little sonatina was in G major and had been marked at the very beginning with an F-sharp; this meant that you could not just comfortably drift along on the white keys, but that at certain points, without any warning in the score, you had to hit one of the black keys, the F-sharp in fact, which can be found just below the G. When the F-sharp appeared in my score for the first time, I did not recognize it for what it was, promptly hit the wrong key, that is, the F, which, as every friend of music will immediately understand, resulted in a jarring dissonance.

"Typical!" Miss Funkel snapped, and stopped short. "Typical! The first minor difficulty and the gentleman promptly plunks the wrong key. Where are your eyes? F-sharp! There it is, big and bold. So take note of it. And now, once more, from the beginning. One-two-three-four . . ."

I still can't explain, even today, how it happened that I made the same mistake a second time. I suppose I was being so careful *not* to make it, smelling an F-sharp in every note, would have preferred to play nothing but F-sharps, had to force myself not to play F-sharps, not yet, no F-sharp yet . . . until . . . yes, until at the same old spot I once again played an F instead of an F-sharp.

Her face was beet-red in an instant, and she started screeching, "Who would have thought it possible! I said F-sharp, confound it! F-sharp. Don't you know where F-sharp is, you blockhead? There!"—*ping, ping*—and she banged at the black key just below the G with her forefinger, its tip hammered to the size of a nickel after decades of lessons. "*This* is an F-sharp!"—*ping, ping*—"*This* is—*"* And at that moment she had to sneeze. She sneezed, quickly wiped her moustache with the aforementioned forefinger, and banged away another two or three times on the key, screeching loudly, "*This* is an F-sharp, *this* is an F-sharp!" Then she pulled her handkerchief from her cuff and blew her nose.

But I stared at the F-sharp, and turned pale. Sticking to the front end of the key was a wriggly-worm, about as long as a fingernail and as thick as a pencil, a shiny greenish-yellow sample of fresh, slimy snot—apparently a product of Miss Funkel's nose—which had been transferred to her moustache as she sneezed, to her forefinger as she wiped her nose, and from her forefinger to the F-sharp.

"Once again now, from the beginning!" a voice growled beside me. "One-two-three-four . . ." And we began to play.

I count the next thirty seconds as among the most terrifying of my life. I could feel the blood rushing from my cheeks and sweat breaking out on my neck. My hair stood on end, my ears turned hot, then cold, then finally were as deaf as if they had been plugged, I could barely hear Anton Diabelli's pretty melody, which I played mechanically now, not even looking at the notes, my fingers moving all on their own after the second repeat—I stared with huge eyes at the slender black key just below the G, and pasted on it, Maria Louisa Funkel's booger . . . another seven measures, now six . . . I couldn't possibly touch the key without landing in the middle of the snot . . . only five now, four . . . but if I didn't hit the key and played an F instead of an F-sharp for the third time, then . . . another three measures—oh please, dear God, perform a miracle! Say something, do something. Let the earth open up! Smash the piano! Make time run backward, so I don't have to play this F-sharp! . . . another two measures, now just one . . . But the good Lord was silent and did nothing, and the last dreadful measure was here, containing—I still remember it exactly—six eighth notes, descending from D to F-sharp, and ending in a G quarter note just above it. My fingers descended the eighth-note stairs as if into Hades, D-C-B-A-G . . . "F-sharp!" a voice screeched beside me . . . and with a clear, pure awareness of what I was about to do and with perfect disdain for death, I played the F.

I was able to pull my fingers away from the keyboard just in time before the cover slammed shut. At the same moment Miss Funkel shot into the air like a jack-in-the-box.

"You did that intentionally!" she bellowed, her voice cracking, so shrill and loud that my deaf ears heard it as a kind of tinkling. "You did that quite intentionally, you rotten little rapscallion! You snot-nosed, pig-headed brat! You impudent scal-awag, you . . ."

And now she began stomping wildly around the table in the middle of the room, banging her fist on the tabletop at every other word.

"But you're not going to lead me around by the nose! Don't think you can get away with this! I'll call your mother. I'll call your father. I'll demand you be given such a whipping that you won't sit for a week. I'll demand you be grounded for three weeks and that you practice nothing but G-major scales three hours every day, and D-major and A-major, too, with F-sharps and C-sharps and G-sharps, until you can play them in your sleep. You'll find out what it means to tangle with me, my

boy, will you ever . . . but what I'd really like to do
. . . with my own bare hands . . . is . . ."

She was so furious that her voice gave out. She
flailed the air with both arms. Her face was purple
now, she looked as if she would burst any moment.
Finally she picked up an apple from the fruit bowl,
hauled back, and flung it with such force against
the wall that it ended up as a lump of brown
applesauce next to the grandfather clock, just
above the turtle head of her old mother.

As if someone had pressed a button, something
ghostly stirred inside the mound of tulle, and an
ancient hand emerged from the folds of the gar-
ment, drifted mechanically to the right, toward the
cookies. . . .

But only I saw it, Miss Funkel didn't even
notice. She flung open the door, pointed with an
outstretched arm, and screeched, "Pack your
things and go!" As I tumbled out the door, she
slammed it loudly behind me.

I was shaking all over. My knees were so wobbly
I could hardly walk, let alone ride a bike. With
trembling hands, I clamped my music into the rack

and started walking my bike. And as I pushed it along, dark thoughts seethed within my soul. What upset and tormented me, until I felt chilled to the bone, was not Miss Funkel's outburst, not her threat to have me whipped and grounded, not the fear of anything. It was, rather, the shock of realizing that the whole world was nothing but one great, unfair, mean, disgusting, wretched place. And other people were to blame for this vile state of affairs. And I mean all of them. Every single person, no exceptions. Beginning with my mother, who wouldn't buy me a decent bike; my father, who always agreed with her; my brother and my sister, who sneered and laughed at my having to ride my bike standing up; and Mrs. Hartlaub's vicious little mutt, who was always chasing me; the pedestrians who thronged Shore Road, so that I couldn't help but be late; Hassler the composer, who bored and badgered me with his fugues; Miss Funkel with her lying accusations and her repulsive booger on the F-sharp . . . even the good Lord himself, yes, the so-called good Lord, who, when you *really* needed Him and pleaded for help, had nothing better to do than wrap Himself in cowardly silence and let fate take its course. What did I need the whole lot of them for, when they were all conspiring against me? What did I care about a world like that? I had no use for such a wretched world. Let them all choke on their own meanness! And smear snot on anything they liked! But count me out! I wasn't going to play their game any longer. I would say farewell to this world. I would commit suicide. Right now.

And the moment the idea came to me, my heart felt light again. There was something so uncommonly comforting and satisfying about the idea that all I needed to do was "depart this life"—as people amiably called the process—and in one fell swoop I'd be done with all the meanness and injustice. My tears dried up. The shaking had stopped. There was hope again. But it had to be soon. Right away. Before I thought better of it.

I climbed onto the pedals and rode off. When I got to the center of Upper Lake, I didn't take Shore Road home but turned to the right, onto a bumpy country lane that headed uphill through the woods and brought me out at the road from school, near the transformer shed. The tallest tree I knew, a mighty old red fir, grew there. My plan was to climb this tree and throw myself from the top. I couldn't have imagined any other way to die. I knew, of course, that you could drown, stab, hang, suffocate, or electrocute yourself—my brother had described the last method to me once in great detail. "But you need a ground," he had said, "that's essential, nothing happens without a ground, otherwise all the birds sitting on electrical lines would drop off dead as doornails. But they don't. And why not? Because they don't have a ground. Theoretically, you can hang on to a high-tension wire with a hundred thousand volts, and nothing will happen—if you don't have a ground." According to my brother. But that was all too complicated for me—electricity and the like. Besides, I didn't know what a ground was. No—my only choice was to fall from a tree. I had experience in falling. Falling didn't scare me. It was the one appropriate means for me to depart this life.

I left my bike beside the transformer shed and

fought my way through the underbrush to the red fir. It was so old that it had no lower branches. I would have to climb a smaller fir nearby and then swing across from there. After that it would be easy. The thick boughs provided a good grip, it was almost like climbing skyward on a ladder, and I didn't stop until light broke through the branches overhead and the trunk was so thin that I could feel it swaying slightly. I was still a little way from the top, but when I looked down for the first time now, I couldn't see the ground anymore; a network of green and brown needles and branches and cones was spread like a thick carpet beneath my feet. No way I could jump from here. It would have been like leaping from above the clouds onto a nearby deceptively solid bed, only to tumble to nowhere. But I didn't want to tumble into nowhere, I wanted to see where I was falling and how. My fall was to be a free-fall, as per Galileo's laws of falling bodies.

And so I climbed back down into dusky regions, circling the trunk as I moved down from bough to bough, gazing below for a hole to open up for a free-fall. A few branches farther down I found it:

an ideal flight path, a vertical shaft directly to the ground, where the tree's gnarled roots would guarantee a hard and absolutely fatal impact. All I had to do was slide away from the trunk and out onto the branch, just a little, and jump, and I would fall unhindered to the earth below.

I slowly bent my knees, sat down on the branch, leaned against the trunk, and caught my breath. Until that moment I was so preoccupied with carrying out the deed that I had not bothered to consider what I was actually about to do. But now, just before the crucial moment, thoughts pressed in on me again, and after cursing and damning this evil world and all its inhabitants one last time, I steered my thoughts in the much more reassuring direction of my own funeral. Oh, it would be a splendid funeral! The church bells would toll, the organ would surge, the cemetery in Upper Lake would barely be able to hold the crowd of mourners. I would be lying in a glass coffin on a bed of flowers, a black pony would pull the hearse, and the only sound would be loud sobbing. My parents were sobbing, and my sister and brother, the kids from my class were sobbing, Mrs. Hart-laub and Miss Funkel were sobbing, relatives and friends had come from far and wide to sob, and they all beat their breasts as they sobbed, and burst into lamentations and called out: "Oh! It is our fault that this dear and special person is no longer with us. Oh! If only we had treated him better, if only we hadn't been mean and unfair to him, he would still be alive, this good, this dear, this special, friendly boy!" At the edge of my grave stood Caroline Kueckelmann, and she threw me a bouquet and at the very last moment burst into tears and cried out in her husky, pain-racked voice: "Oh, my dearest! You were so special! If only I had walked with you that Monday."

What marvelous fantasies! I wallowed in them, I played funeral over and over in new variations, from the wake to the feast that followed, where they praised me in lovely eulogies, until finally I was so moved by it all that tears came to my eyes, although I did not sob. It was the most beautiful funeral anyone in our town had ever seen, and decades later people would still remember it

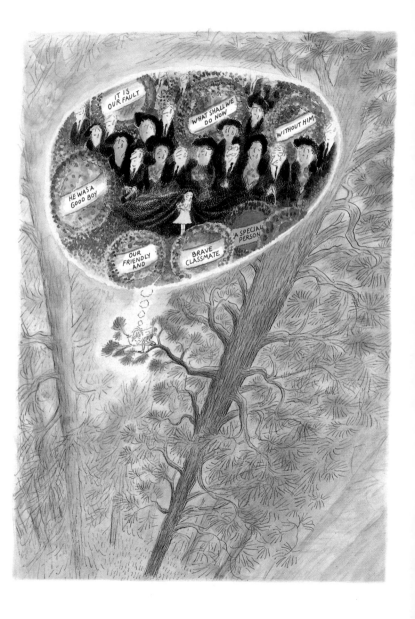

wistfully and talk about it. What a rotten shame I wouldn't actually be able to join in—because I would be dead then. No doubt about that, sad to say. I would *have* to be dead for my own funeral. You couldn't have both at the same time: taking your revenge *on* the world and going on living *in* the world. And so, revenge it was!

I loosened my hold on the trunk. Slowly I inched my way out, still holding on to the trunk with my right hand, half bracing, half pushing, while grasping tightly with my left to the branch I was sitting on. Then came the moment when I was touching the trunk with only my fingertips . . . and then not even with my fingertips . . . and there I sat, with nothing to hold on to except the branch, which I clutched tightly in both hands—free as a bird, the depths below me. Very, very cautiously I looked down. I estimated my height above the ground at about three times the height of the highest gable on our house, which was thirty-three feet. That made ninety-nine feet. According to Galileo's laws of falling bodies, that meant the fall I was about to experience would last exactly

2.4730986 seconds,* and that my speed at the time of impact would be 54.27 miles per hour.†

I looked down for a long time. The depths tempted me. They lured me seductively. They seemed to wave and call, "Come, come!" They tugged at invisible threads, "Come, come!" And it was easy. Easy as pie. Just lean forward the least bit, until you were just slightly off balance—and the rest would take care of itself. . . . "Come, come!"

Yes! I want to, I do! I just can't decide when. I can't decide the precise moment, the exact point in time. I can't seem to say, "Now! I'll do it now!"

I decided to count to three, the way we did for

---

*Discounting air resistance!

†Of course, I didn't do the calculation to seven places after the decimal at the time, sitting out there on the branch, but only much, much later, with the help of a pocket calculator. At the time, I knew about the laws of falling bodies only from hearing people mention them, but I did not know their actual meaning or the mathematical formulas. My calculations that day were limited to estimating the height and guessing, on the basis of various empirical experiences, that it would be a relatively long fall and that my speed at the time of impact would be very fast, relatively speaking.

races or when we jumped into the water, and at 'three' I'd let go. I took a deep breath and counted:

"One . . . two . . ." And then I stopped again, because I didn't know whether I should jump with my eyes open or closed. After brief consideration, I decided to count with my eyes closed, lean forward into the void at "three," eyes still closed, but at the moment I began to fall, to open them again. I closed my eyes and counted: "One . . . two . . ."

Then I heard a knocking sound. It was coming from the road. A hard, rhythmical knock, *tock-tock-tock-tock*, at a tempo double my own counting: there was a *tock* at "one," then a *tock* between "one" and "two," at "two," and after "two" and just before I got to "three"—just like Miss Funkel's metronome. *Tock-tock-tock-tock.* It almost seemed as if the sound were mocking my own counting. I opened my eyes, and the knocking stopped, and all I heard now was rustling, snapping twigs, and the vigorous panting of some animal—and suddenly there was Mr. Summer directly under me, ninety-nine feet below, so that if I had jumped now I would have smashed not only myself, but him as well. I clutched my branch tightly and didn't move.

Mr. Summer stood there, stock-still, and panted. Once he had caught his breath a little, he suddenly held it for a moment and turned his head in a jerky motion in all directions, listening, I suppose. Then he ducked down and looked under the bushes on his left, into the underbrush on his right, crept around the tree trunk like an Indian, returned to the same spot, listened and stared in all directions once more (but not above him!), and having made certain that no one was following him, that there was no one anywhere in the vicinity, he tossed his straw hat, staff, and backpack on the ground with three rapid motions, and stretched out among the roots of the woodland floor as if it were a bed. But he did not lie easy in his bed, because no sooner had he lain down than he let out a long, dreadful sigh—no, not a sigh, there's some relief in a sigh, it was more a moan, a mournful groan from deep in his chest, mixing despair and a longing for relief. And then a second time, the same hair-raising sound, the same pleading groan, like a patient in painful agony—and still no relief, no rest, not a moment of repose. Instead, he was already sitting up again, and he grabbed for his backpack, hastily pulled out his sandwich and a flat tin canteen, and began to eat, no, to devour his sandwich, stuffing it down and gazing mistrustfully all around after each bite, as if enemies were lurking in the woods, as if some horrible pursuer were right behind and the brief head start he had on him were growing shorter and shorter and the pursuer would appear here, at this very spot, at any moment. The sandwich was gone in no time, chased down by a quick swallow from the canteen, and then came hectic haste and a panicky departure: canteen tossed into the backpack, backpack shouldered as he stood up, staff and hat snatched up in one grab, and off he went, striding through the bushes—panting, cracking twigs, and then from the road, moving rapidly away, the metronome knock of his staff on the hard asphalt: *Tock-tock-tock-tock-tock . . .*

I was sitting in the fork of the branch, clinging to the trunk of the fir—I don't know how I got there. I was trembling. I was cold. I suddenly had no urge whatever to jump to the depths below. That seemed ridiculous now. I no longer understood how I could have come up with such an idiotic idea: to kill myself because of a booger! And here I had just seen a man who, his whole life long, had been fleeing from death.

It was perhaps five or six years before I met up with Mr. Summer the next, and last, time. I had seen him frequently during that period; it would have been nearly impossible not to see him, since he was constantly under way, whether on main roads or on the numerous little paths around the lake, or out in the fields and woods. But I paid him no particular attention, and I suppose no one paid him any particular attention, they had seen him so often that they overlooked him, like some all too familiar item in the landscape, not the sort of thing to make you cry out in amazement every time you see it: "Look, the steeple! Look, there's School Hill! Look, there goes the bus!" At most, if I was riding with my father to the Sunday races and we happened to pass him, we might joke and say, "Look, there goes Mr. Summer—he'll catch his death!" But we weren't really referring to him, only to our own recollection of the hailstorm that day many,

many years before, when my father had used that cliché.

It was general knowledge that his wife, the doll-maker, had died, but no one knew exactly when or where, and no one had attended the funeral. He no longer lived in the Stanglmeiers' basement—the housepainter's daughter Rita lived there now with her husband—but a few houses farther down, in the attic of Riedl the fisherman. But he was very seldom at home, as Mrs. Riedl noted later, and if so, then only for a short time; just for a bite to eat or a cup of tea, and then he was on his way again. He often didn't come home for days, not even to sleep; but where he spent his nights, or if he even bothered to stop somewhere to sleep rather than wander about as he did during the day, no one knew. And no one cared, either. People had other problems now. They worried about their cars, their washing machines, their lawn sprinklers, but not about where some old eccentric laid his head. They talked about what they had heard the day before on the radio or seen on television or about Mrs. Hirt's new self-service grocery—but not about

Mr. Summer. Even though people might spot him once in a while, Mr. Summer was no longer on their minds. The times, as they say, had slipped right past Mr. Summer.

But not me! I had kept up with the times. I was very much up-to-date—at least so it seemed to me—and sometimes I felt as if I were even ahead of my time. I was almost five-foot-seven, weighed one hundred eight pounds, and wore men's size-seven shoes. I was about to enter my sophomore year in high school. I had read all the fairy tales of the Brothers Grimm, and half of Maupassant, too. I had already smoked half a cigarette and had seen two movies about the life of an Austrian empress. It would not be long until my student ID would be stamped with the much-coveted "over 16," which would entitle me to see adult films and frequent taverns until ten p.m. without "accompanying parents and/or guardians." I could solve equations with three unknowns, had built my own crystal set and could get AM stations on it, could recite by heart the opening of *De bello gallico* and the first line of the *Odyssey*, although I had never learned a word of Greek. I no longer played Diabelli or the odious Hassler, but, along with blues and boogie-woogie, renowned composers like Haydn, Schumann, Beethoven, and Chopin, and stoically endured Miss Funkel's occasional rages, usually with a secret grin.

I hardly ever climbed trees. But I did have my own bike by then, my brother's old three-speed racer, on which I broke the old record of thirteen and a half minutes from Lower Lake to the Villa Funkel by no less than thirty-five seconds, arriving in twelve minutes, fifty-five seconds—timed on my own wristwatch. I was—in all modesty—a brilliant cyclist, not just in terms of speed and stamina, but also in terms of skill. Riding no-handed, even around curves, turning circles at a standstill by braking and whirling the bike around on one wheel—these presented no problem at all. I could even stand on the back rack with the bike in motion—a pointless but artistically impressive achievement, an eloquent witness to my trust in the conservation of rotational impulse, a trust that was in fact boundless by now. My skepticism about

bike-riding, both in theory and practice, had vanished completely. I was an enthusiastic biker. Riding a bike was almost like flying.

To be sure, there were some things during this epoch in my life to sour my existence, in particular (a) the fact that at the time I did not have access to an FM radio, and so was forced to miss my favorite detective series, on Thursday evenings from ten to eleven, and for better or worse—usually worse—wait until the next morning for my friend Cornelius Michel to tell me about it; and (b) the fact that we did not own a television set. "I will not have a television set in my house," decreed my father, who was born in the same year that Giuseppe Verdi died, "because television puts an end to musical evenings at home, ruins your eyes, destroys family life, and ultimately leads to general idiocy."* Unfortunately, my mother did not argue

*There was only one day in the year when television did not ruin your eyes or lead to general idiocy, and that was a day in early July when the German Derby was broadcast from the thoroughbred track at Hamburg-Horn. On that occasion my father would put on his gray top hat, drive to the Michels' in Upper Lake, and watch the race from there.

with him on this point, and so I had to put up with my friend Cornelius Michel in order to have access to such important cultural events as *I Remember Mama, Lassie,* and *The Adventures of Hiram Holliday.*

It was my bad luck that almost all of these programs were in the so-called early prime-time slot and ended at eight on the dot with the national news. I was supposed to be home, sitting at the dinner table with hands washed, by eight on the dot. But since you cannot be in two places at one time, particularly when those places are separated by a bike ride of seven and a half minutes—and that's not counting the hand-washing—my television escapades regularly led to a classic conflict between duty and desire. Either I would leave for home seven and a half minutes before the program ended—and miss the unraveling of the dramatic knot; or I would stay till the end, which meant arriving seven and a half minutes late for dinner and risking a row with my mother and a lengthy, triumphant exposition by my father about television's destructive effect on family life. It seems to me that that phase of my life was defined by conflicts of this or a similar sort. It was always the same; you *had* to, should, should not, really had best do this or that; there was always something they expected, demanded, ordered you to do: Do this! Do that! And don't forget that! Did you take care of that? Did you stop by there yet? Why did you wait till now? . . . Constant pressure, stress, and never enough time, someone always pointing to a clock. You were seldom left in peace, in those days. . . . But I don't want to wander off into great laments, expatiating on the conflicts of my adolescence. I would do better to scratch the back of my head, maybe tap softly on that one special spot a few times with my middle finger, and concentrate on what I apparently would rather avoid: an account of my last meeting with Mr. Summer, which is also the end of his and of my story.

It was in autumn, after another such evening of television with Cornelius Michel. The program had been boring, you could guess how it would end, and so I left the Michels' at five till eight, intending to arrive home for dinner more or less on time.

Darkness had definitely settled over the land, with a trace of gray lingering only in the west, above the lake. I rode without a light, first because my light was constantly on the fritz—it was the bulb or the switch or the cable—and second because when I turned on the generator it slowed my coasting speed considerably, adding more than a minute to the trip to Lower Lake. I didn't need a light anyway. I could have ridden this stretch in my sleep. Even on the blackest night, the asphalt on the narrow road was always a little blacker than the fences on one side and the bushes on the other, so that you needed to steer only where it was blackest and you would be right on course.

And so I raced through the oncoming night, bent low over the handlebars, in third gear, wind whistling in my ears; it was cool, damp, now and then you smelled smoke.

Almost exactly halfway home—at this point the road curved gently away from the lake toward an old gravel pit, the woods looming up behind—my chain slipped out. Sad to say, this was a fairly frequent problem with my gearshift, which func-

tioned flawlessly otherwise—the result of a worn spring that made the chain run slack. I had spent long afternoons trying to fix the problem, but to no avail. So I stopped, got off, and bent down over the back wheel to tug at the chain and free it from where it was caught between the freewheel and the frame and then feed it back onto the teeth by gently rotating the pedals. I was so familiar with this procedure that I could do it even in the dark without difficulty. The trouble was that you ended up with disgustingly greasy fingers. And so after I had refitted the chain, I walked across to the lake side of the road to wipe my hands on the large, dry leaves of a young maple. When I pulled down the branch, I had a free view to the lake. It lay there like a big bright mirror. And at the edge of the mirror stood Mr. Summer.

At first I thought he wasn't wearing shoes. But then I realized he was standing in water up over his boots, a few yards from the shore, his back to me, gazing toward the west, to the far shore and the few last whitish-yellow rays of light behind the mountains. He stood there like a fencepost, a dark

silhouette against the bright mirror of the lake, his long, sinuous staff in his right hand, his straw hat on his head.

And then suddenly he began to move. Step by step, planting his staff firmly and shoving off against it with every third step, Mr. Summer walked into the lake. Walked as if he were on dry land, in his typical resolute haste, walked out into the middle of the lake, heading due west. The lake is shallow at this point, and gets deeper only very gradually. After he had gone about sixty feet, the water still came up only to his hips, and when it finally reached his chest, he was farther out than you could have thrown a stone. And kept walking, his haste retarded now by the water, but still resolute, without the least hesitation, stubborn, eager, it seemed, to move even faster through the barrier of water—until at last he threw his staff away and began to row with his arms.

I stood on the shore and stared at him, my eyes wide, my mouth open; I imagine I must have looked like someone being told a fascinating story. I wasn't frightened but, rather, amazed by what I saw, entranced, though admittedly without quite comprehending the awfulness of what was happening. At first I thought: He's just standing there looking for something he lost in the water; but who wears boots into the water to look for something? Then, as he began to march off, I thought: He's going for a dip; but who does that fully dressed, at night, in October? And finally, as he walked out into deeper and deeper water, the absurd thought came to me that he wanted to walk across the lake—not to swim it, swimming didn't occur to me at all, Mr. Summer and swimming, that was a contradiction; no, he would cross the lake on foot, hurrying across the bottom, three hundred feet underwater, all three miles to the far shore.

Now the water was up to his shoulders, up to his neck . . . and he kept pressing forward, out into the lake . . . and now he rose up again, grew, lifted apparently by some irregularity of the bottom, and his shoulders were above water again . . . and kept walking, not stopping, not even now, kept walking and sank lower again, up to his neck, his Adam's apple, his chin . . . and only now did I begin to suspect what he was doing, but I didn't move, didn't call out: "Mr. Summer! Wait! Come back!" didn't run off to get help, didn't look around for a boat or a raft or an air mattress, anything to rescue him; in fact I didn't allow myself to blink as I watched the little dot of his head sink out there.

And then, all at once, it was gone. Only the straw hat still floated on the water. And after a dreadfully long time, maybe half a minute, maybe a whole minute, a few large bubbles rose up, then nothing more. Except for that ridiculous hat, which slowly floated off to the southwest. I watched for a long time, until it vanished in the dusky distance.

III

T wo weeks went by before anyone even noticed Mr. Summer's disappearance. The first person to notice was Mrs. Riedl, the fisherman's wife, who was worried about the rent due on the room in the attic. And when Mr. Summer still did not show up after two more weeks, she said something about it to Mrs. Stanglmeier, and Mrs. Stanglmeier said something to Mrs. Hirt, who then asked her customers. But since no one had seen Mr. Summer or knew anything about where he might be, Mr. Riedl waited another two weeks and then decided to file a missing-person's report with the police, and several weeks later a brief notice appeared in the local paper, with an ancient passport photo, which no one would ever have recognized as Mr. Summer, since it showed him as a young man with a full head of black hair, keen eyes, and a confident, almost impudent smile on his lips. And under the photograph, people read

Mr. Summer's full name for the first time: Maximilian Ernest Aegidius Summer.

For a brief while, then, Mr. Summer and his mysterious disappearance were the talk of the village. "He's gone completely mad," some people said, "he's gotten lost and can't find his way home. Probably doesn't even remember his own name or address."

"Maybe he's emigrated," others said, "to Canada or Australia. Maybe, with his claustrophobia, Europe has gotten too crowded for him."

"He got lost in the mountains and fell to his death in a ravine," still others said.

No one thought of the lake. And before the newspaper had even turned yellow, Mr. Summer was forgotten. After all, no one missed him. Mrs. Riedl moved his few belongings to one corner in the cellar and rented the attic room from then on to summer guests. Although she never said "summer guests," because that seemed an odd expression to her. She called them "city folks" or "tourists."

And I said nothing. Not a word. Even that same

evening, when I arrived home later than usual and had to listen to a lecture on the destructive effects of television, I did not say one word about what I knew. And not later on, either. Not to my sister, not to my brother, not to the police, not even to Cornelius Michel—I didn't breathe a word of it. . . .

I'm not sure why I persisted in keeping silent for so long . . . but I don't think it was fear or guilt or even a bad conscience. It was the memory of that groan in the woods, of those trembling lips in the rain, of those pleading words: "Why can't you just leave me in peace!"—the same memory that kept me from saying anything as I watched Mr. Summer sink into the lake.

A Note About the Author

Patrick Süskind was born in Ambach, near Munich, in 1949. He studied medieval and modern history at the University of Munich. His first novel, *Perfume,* was an internationally acclaimed best seller. Mr. Suskind lives and writes in Munich.

A Note About the Illustrator

Jean-Jacques Sempé was born in Bordeaux in 1932 and now lives in Paris. His drawings were first published in *Paris Match* when he was nineteen. For many years he worked for the weekly magazine *L'Express.* Today he concentrates on publishing books of his watercolors and drawings. His most recent book was *Par Avion.*

A Note About the Type

The text of this book was set in a digitized version of Centaur. Originally designed by Bruce Rogers in 1914 as a private type, it was named for the book in which it was first used (*The Centaur* by Maurice de Guérin). Monotype made it generally available in 1929.

Rogers based his design upon the 1470 font of Nicolas Jenson, the Venetian printer, introducing refinements lacking in the original. Typographers consider Centaur to be one of the finest roman types currently available, a superb revival of the Jenson letter which has served as an inspiration for all designers of roman type.

Composed by The Sarabande Press, New York, New York
Printed and Bound by
Impresora Donneco International,
a division of R. R. Donnelley & Sons,
Reynosa, Mexico

Designed by Mia Vander Els